The Runner

If you enjoyed reading this book, you might also like to try another story from the **Mammoth Read** series:

illustrated by Clive Scruton

The Runner

Keith Gray

mammoth

For absent friends: Andy Briggs,
Brother Dave, Bub and Dr Nozza
KG

First published in Great Britain in 1998
by Mammoth, an imprint of Egmont Children's Books Limited
a division of Egmont Holding Limited
239 Kensington High Street, London W8 6SA

Text copyright © 1998 Keith Gray
Illustrations copyright © 1998 Clive Scruton
Cover illustration © 2001 Mark Edwards

The moral rights of the author, illustrator, and cover illustrator have
been asserted.

ISBN 0 7497 4555 X

10 9 8 7 6 5 4

Printed in Great Britain by Cox & Wyman Ltd., Reading, Berkshire

Contents

1 *The monster Intercity*

IT WASN'T RUNNING away. Not proper running away. Not really.

The monster Intercity hauled itself into the station. Jason was already at the edge of the platform with his bag in his hand. The other waiting passengers crowded round him as the train slowed. He kept his head low, scared someone might recognise him, and gripped the handles of his bag tighter. It felt so very heavy, it seemed to be dragging him down. Could he really carry it all the way

to Liverpool? After as many as eight or nine carriages the train finally managed to bring itself to a halt. It still had another two or three to go but left them hanging out of the station, like a tall man in a small bed. The straggly crowd was an excuse not to queue and Jason was the last to climb aboard, even though he'd been one of the first waiting.

He followed the crowd on to the train and grabbed the first empty seat he came to. Then almost immediately wished he hadn't. Sitting across the aisle from him was an elderly woman with a bag of Mint Imperials and a wrinkly smile. She offered him first the smile, then a sweet. He shook his head quickly and hurried through to the next carriage along, lugging his bag behind him. The woman looked just like his Auntie Jen, who Michael had always called the nosiest woman in the world. But this carriage was better, just some businessmen who seemed far too interested in their morning papers to wonder what an eleven-year-old boy was doing travelling so far by himself.

He sat by the window and let his bag block the seat next to him. He checked his watch. Nine twenty-seven; the train left at half past. He was surprised by just how hard and fast his heart was beating and zipped his jacket right up under his chin to try to help keep the noise in, then folded his arms over his chest too.

He began humming a tune to himself nervously. At first he thought he was making it up. He hated himself when he realised it was one of the songs that his father always played and forced it quickly out of his head. He thought of something by Oasis instead, because they were Michael's favourite band, and waited for the train to get going.

From his window seat he could see along the train tracks, out of the station. He followed them into the distance with his eyes. It was strange to think they eventually joined up to Liverpool. If he was strong enough, would he be able to pull on them like ropes and drag Liverpool, and Michael, closer to him?

He fidgeted in his seat, not feeling

comfortable. He dug in his coat pocket for a stick of chewing-gum, but didn't have one. He chewed on his lip instead, and wished the train would hurry up and get going.

Nine twenty-eight. Miss Hill would have taken the register by now. She'd know he wasn't at school. He realised he was sitting facing in the wrong direction to be able to see the entrance to the train station, or the footbridge across the tracks. He was itching to turn round and look, the feeling prickled and plucked at the hair on the back of his neck, but he was scared he'd give himself away if he did. He'd told Ben he was going to the dentist, and could only hope his friend had shouted this information out when Miss Hill had called his name. But what if he hadn't? And what if they'd guessed?

Nine twenty-nine. Jason folded his arms tighter until he was almost hugging himself. He willed the train to get going. What if they told his Mum and Dad? If the train would just hurry up and get going. What if they called the police?

He stood up slowly, watching the businessmen all the time to see if they were watching him. He lifted his bag up to push it on to the high rack. He struggled a little, his hands shaking, but was able to stare up and down the station in both directions. And thankfully there wasn't a policeman or parent in sight.

He sat back down, arms folded again. Feeling better, but not that great. Still nine twenty-nine. He wished he'd stayed standing, waited that little bit longer, just in case. Because his mum could be there right now, behind his back. And his dad could be running across the footbridge.

But the train gave a little jolt. Then a shudder. Slowly it began to move alongside the platform. The waiting-room slipped smoothly away.

'Good,' Jason said aloud. No stopping me now, he

told himself. No turning back. But he found the thought oddly unsettling. It made his stomach bubble and fizz worse than a glass of lemonade.

2 *No turning back*

THE TRAIN PUSHED past the houses and hurried on into the open fields. It dashed over a level-crossing with a short queue of cars and trees on either

side. Jason was still fidgeting in his seat, still worried someone might ask him just what on earth he thought he was doing missing double history this morning. He didn't know whether to keep his head down low enough to hide his face, or sit up straight to be able to keep a look out.

His parents had argued again last night. And the shouting had been so loud

he'd been scared the old couple next door would be able to hear. Well, he told himself, they could argue as loud as they wanted now that he wasn't there.

A short, bald businessman with a Bugs

Bunny tie got up from his seat and started walking towards Jason. The man was staring straight at him. And his heart suddenly picked up enough speed to be able to race the train. He was certain the man recognised him, no doubt about it. He shrank down low in his seat as the man came closer, fearing the worst. Was he a friend of his parents? A teacher? A

neighbour? Was he? But the man carried on up the aisle, he didn't even slow. Jason swivelled in his seat to watch him go, still suspicious, until the businessman was through into the previous carriage and heading for the buffet. Only then did he turn back to face in the right direction and try to get his heart to slow down a little.

Michael had moved away the day after his eighteenth birthday. Before that he'd always been there to help with homework. He'd always been there to help with Gary Morgan when he was picking on the smaller kids. And he'd always been there to play his music loud when their mum and dad were fighting. Things hadn't

exactly changed since Michael had left home, they'd just got worse. Because Jason was alone now.

He fidgeted some more, he wanted the toilet. It was maybe the orange juice that his mother had forced him to drink for breakfast, although he supposed that it was probably his nerves as well. He wanted to go pretty badly, but forced himself to stay put until the man with the Bugs Bunny tie returned to his seat. He kept checking over his shoulder, watching for him. He wanted to make sure he definitely didn't recognise him.

The train raced through a narrow, tree-lined cutting and into a tunnel. Jason could see his face reflected in the dark window. He thought about how his mum and dad were going to react when he didn't come home tonight. About what the teachers, and Ben, and the other kids at school were going to say. Would he ever

be able to tell them the truth? He wasn't simply visiting his brother. He was travelling all this way because deep down he hoped he would never have to go back to the unhappiness of his home.

At last the man with the Bugs Bunny tie reappeared. He was carrying a steaming cup of coffee. Jason watched him very carefully, examining his face. Only when

he was sure the man was a stranger could
he relax. But he'd have to keep a close eye
on him anyway. Just in case.

3 *Meeting Jam*

HE MADE HIS way down the aisle towards the toilet, double-checking the other passengers, but thankfully there was no one else he recognised. He was swaying slightly with the rocking motion of the high-speed train. The juice he'd had for breakfast sloshed around in his stomach, making him want to hurry. He had a strange thought that although he was walking against the train, in the opposite direction to the way it was travelling, it was still carrying him closer and closer to Liverpool.

The toilet was engaged. He stood in the noisy corridor between the two carriages and gritted his teeth impatiently. He could really hear the speed of the train here, its rip-roaring, headlong progress cross-country, and could feel its rumble beneath his feet. He wanted to knock on the locked door. He kept glanc-

ing up and down the train, peering into the carriages on either side. He knew he was standing in full view of both the man with the Bugs Bunny tie as well as the old woman with the bag of Mint Imperials, and it was making him nervous again.

When the toilet door was suddenly yanked open it made him jump slightly, he'd been so lost in his worries. He was

more than a little shocked when a young boy's head appeared round the edge of the door. The boy looked equally surprised himself. They stared at each other in silence for a second or two, then the boy looked quickly up and down the noisy corridor, almost copying exactly what Jason had been doing.

'Has he been yet? Have you seen him?

He must have gone past by now. Must
have. We're nearly at Sheffield, aren't
we?' The boy's words clattered along at
about the same speed as the train. He
looked at Jason expectantly. But Jason
had no idea what on earth he was
talking about.

The boy looked up and down the
corridor again, then back at Jason.

'What's up? You got the cat's tongue, yeah? Can't talk?'

Jason shook his head and shrugged. 'I don't,' he started, but didn't stand a chance of finishing.

'The conductor. Has he gone yet? Haven't got a ticket, you see? Didn't buy one. Sneaked on. Stowaway. Can't let him see me. He'll kick me off, won't he?'

The words clogged up Jason's ears as if they were all trying to push inside at the same time and kept getting stuck. All he could do was shake his head again.

'I see him, I see him! He's coming!' The boy's bright blue eyes went wide, and Jason turned to look down the train with him. But before he had a chance to do anything, the boy grabbed him by the front of his coat and dragged him inside the toilet cubicle.

'Hey!' Jason tried to fight the boy's grip.

'Shush! Shut up, can't you? D'you wanna get me kicked off, or what?' He pushed Jason down on to the closed toilet seat and squeezed up against him. 'He'd love to kick me off, this one. Burkey. Jerky Burkey. Burke the jerk. Been after me for months, yeah?' He let Jason go, but was still standing close enough to block the door. 'Hey?' he asked suddenly, 'You're not a Runner as well are you?'

Jason shook his head, not that he knew exactly what a Runner was.

'Didn't think so. Hey! Shush, shush. He's coming. Shush then.'

The boy wasn't as tall as Jason, but was certainly a lot heavier. His weight pushed down on him in the cramped cubicle. He was a small and stocky kid with cropped fair hair; too long to be a crew cut, but too short to be anything else.

Jason squirmed a little, desperate to get up. He still needed to pee.

'Quiet, quiet. Shush then. Shut up.'

He was probably the same age as Jason, just looked older, his voice hadn't broken yet. He was wearing a blue checked shirt with short sleeves and jeans with chunky turn-ups round each ankle. He had a finger to his lips. His nail was bitten about as close as it could be. He had turned away from Jason, head cocked as if listening, looking at the toilet door.

Jason realised the door was still open, and it moved gently with the rocking of the train. He really had no wish to be any part of whatever trouble this boy was in, but didn't want to get caught by the conductor trapped in the toilet with him either. He didn't want anybody asking too many questions.

'The door's still open,' he whispered.

'Leave it. Doesn't matter.' The boy shook his head. 'You should never close it. He knows you're in here then, doesn't he? He waits for you outside. Waits for you to come out. Gets you as soon as you –' He was cut short when he heard the hiss of the automatic door from the carriage.

Someone walked by.

Then, with the hiss of the automatic door through into the next carriage, the boy breathed an exaggerated sigh of relief.

'That was close. Bit too close, yeah? Maybe I should get off at Sheffield? Burkey'd love to kick me off again. He can't stand Runners. Especially me. Hates me. Not long to Sheffield, is it?'

'I'm not sure,' Jason admitted.

'Yeah. Not far.' The boy said it more to himself than to Jason. 'Not far at all.' He leaned back, poked his head round the door.

'Right. Thanks. Seeya.' He scarpered in

the opposite direction to the way that the
conductor had gone.

4 *Sheffield and beyond*

WHEN JASON RETURNED to his seat the Intercity was pulling into Sheffield station. He was a third of the way there now, only a stop at

Manchester after this, and then Liverpool. And Michael. He hoped Michael wasn't going to be mad with him for what he was doing. His brother was the only one who understood him, the only one who knew what it was like to live with his parents, and he hated to think about Michael being angry with him. So he pushed the thought to the back of his

mind, it just made his stomach feel funny again.

The further Jason got away from home the less jumpy he felt; the less likely it was someone might recognise him. But the problem was, now that there was no turning back, the train was giving him plenty of time to think about what he was doing. And about the consequences.

He looked out on to the station and craned his neck, peering up and down the platform, wanting to see the boy when he got off. He expected to see him make a dash for the stairs to the exit.

Several people got into Jason's carriage, but the boy didn't appear and the train gradually hauled itself away again. Jason still watched however, and wondered

exactly what a Runner could be. A run-away perhaps? Is that what Jason was?

Once more the houses gave way to the countryside. The great, green hills of the Pennines grew high on either side, misty at the top. It started to rain, droplets shattered against the window. Jason's thoughts drifted back to school. Was he missed yet? Was Ben wondering where he

was? He looked at his watch. Ten fifty-eight. English. Jason liked English. He sat next to Rachel Johnson who looked pretty in her little, round glasses. Her mother and father were divorced, and Jason had often wondered how she coped.

He felt cheated by his own parents, misled. He felt as though they'd lied to him about being happy when he was

younger. He'd tried to check up on this, tried to prove himself wrong. Two nights ago he'd sneaked into their bedroom and stolen the old photograph album from the bottom draw of the dressing-table. He'd checked the smiles in the pictures of past birthdays and holidays but hadn't been quite able to work out how real they looked. He kept the picture of

him and Michael in the swimming-pool at Scarborough. It was a really old one, from when he'd still had braces on his teeth, but it was one of the few he could trust.

5 *Stealing breakfast*

THE COUNTRYSIDE RUSHED past the window. The train was only a quarter of an hour out of Sheffield when the strange boy appeared again.

'Hey,' he said. 'Here a minute. Listen.' He plopped down in the seat next to Jason. 'I need a favour. Give us a hand, yeah?'

Jason wished he'd keep his voice down. He looked round anxiously at the other passengers, scared they'd be watching.

Not that the other boy cared. 'I'm starved,' he said. 'I've not eaten since

yesterday.' He rubbed his belly as if this proved it. 'Help us to get some food, yeah? The bloke with the trolley's coming this way. I just want a couple of Mars or something. They'll keep me going 'til later.'

Jason shrugged. 'I haven't got much money.'

'No.' The boy shook his head. 'No. I don't want your money. I'll get them

myself. I don't need money. You just keep him talking, yeah? And I'll grab something. Quick, like. Before he sees me.'

Jason was shocked. 'I can't do that!'

'Course you can. It's dead easy. No sweat. I've done it loads of times. Simple.'

'But –'

'Watch out, here he comes. See him? See him there?' The boy stood up. 'Just ask him

a couple of prices, yeah? Keep him talking. I'll be real quick.' He moved up the train by several seats, but turned round to keep his eye on Jason. 'Go on. As a favour. We'll scratch our backs together, yeah?' He winked.

Jason watched the attendant in his bright red waistcoat with the refreshment trolley moving slowly along the carriage towards him, struggling with the narrowness of the aisle and the train's steady rocking. He looked around him at the other passengers, a few of whom glanced up at the other boy standing in his seat.

Jason couldn't help him steal. But what would this kid do if he didn't help? What if he really hadn't eaten today?

The trolley squeaked closer and closer down the aisle. The man pulled it along, politely offering drinks and snacks. Little glass bottles tinkled against each other.

The boy was leaning over the back of his seat, watching it coming, watching Jason. Go on, he mouthed silently. Nodding at Jason, winking. Go on.

The attendant passed the boy, who climbed out of his seat to follow him, sneaking along almost theatrically. Jason looked nervously at the other passengers slumped in their seats, staring at newspapers or out of the window. The attendant and his complaining trolley were nearly to him. The boy was stalking it down the aisle, urging Jason on.

'Would you like something to eat?'

Jason stared at the attendant almost
frozen to his seat. Out of the corner of his
eye he could see the boy getting closer
and closer. And somehow he managed to
stutter: 'T-Two Mars bars, please.'

The boy halted mid-pounce. He hopped
into a seat instead of on to the trolley, but
Jason couldn't see the look on his face.

He paid for the Mars bars and thanked
the attendant quickly, his face burning
with a hot blush that matched the man's
red waistcoat.

As soon as the attendant had pulled his
noisy trolley away, the boy appeared and
plopped back into the seat next to
Jason's. 'Chicken,' he said. But ate both
of the Mars bars all the same.

6 *On the run*

'COULDN'T GET OFF at Sheffield,' the boy informed Jason as he crumpled the two empty black wrappers. 'Burkey was too close to the doors, hang-

ing around. He's dead sly, like. He must know I'm here, yeah? He's got a sixth-sense for Runners, that guy.'

Jason was fascinated. He watched him licking the chocolate off his teeth.

'Could do with a drink now. Wash it down. Get that later, yeah? Show you how to steal from the buffet, what d'you reckon?'

Jason simply shrugged.

'My name's Jam. That's what the others call me anyway. I like it, yeah? Who're you?'

'Jason.'

Jam nodded as if he'd guessed that much already. 'Where're you going? Going far, yeah?'

'Liverpool.'

'Yeah? Me too. If I get there.' He looked up and down the carriage, checking for the conductor. Then turned back to Jason. 'So, are you running away or not?'

Jason started nervously. 'No!' he said a little too loudly. 'No. I'm going to visit my brother.'

Jam nodded again. 'Yeah, didn't think

you could be a Runner. You don't look the type, do you?' He got up to leave. 'Well, ta for breakfast and that.' He started to walk away up the train.

Jason watched him, then checked to make sure the other passengers were busy with their papers. The last thing he wanted to do was draw attention to himself, but he was far too curious to let Jam go now.

He hurried to catch him up. 'I'll buy you a drink if you want.'

The other boy shrugged. 'OK,' he said. 'OK. Yeah. Ta.' Then glanced quickly round himself in that furtive manner he had. 'Just have to watch for Burkey, yeah? Keep out of sight, like.' Which was fine by Jason.

Jam led the way to the buffet car in the middle of the train. He always stopped before they entered a different carriage, to make sure the conductor was nowhere in sight. In one of the carriages he nodded and winked at a ginger-haired boy sitting at a table with his parents. The boy looked surprised but returned an

awkward, hesitant smile before turning quickly away.

Jason bought Jam a can of Lilt and got a bag of crisps for himself. They stood in the corridor next to the buffet car. Jam drank the Lilt in two gulps, then picked at the crisps.

'He's a Runner too,' Jam said. 'Tommy Red. The kid I said hiya to. Good idea

that, sitting with a couple of adults. Makes it look like you're theirs, yeah? You don't get asked for your ticket then. And the conductors can't remember everyone, can they? I didn't want to give him away though. I didn't stop to chat.'

Jason let the boy take all of the crisps and asked the question that he'd been burning to ask all along.

'What exactly is a Runner anyway?'

'A Runner? Me. I'm a Runner, yeah? Have been for nearly a year now.' He tipped the crisp packet up into his mouth to get the crumbs from the bottom. Jason waited patiently. Jam patted the bag gently, and shook it. 'I liked them. They were nice,' he said, finally satisfied the packet was empty. He crumpled it in

both hands and dropped it to the floor.

'There's loads of us, all over the place. We live on trains, yeah? Big ones like these. We go across the country all the time. Cross-country runaways, yeah? We call ourselves Runners.'

Jason couldn't tell if he was being lied to or not. 'How do you live on trains?'

'Easy. Especially big ones like these.

You can nearly get lost on these.'

Jason nodded, remembering the size of the monster as it pulled into the station back home. 'And there's lots of you? I mean, lots of Runners?'

'Oh yeah.' Jam nodded his head vigorously. 'Yeah. Loads. You've probably seen us and never known. Kids on their own at stations, they're usually Runners. That's

why I thought you were one. But some do like Tommy Red is doing and follow adults, so they don't look dead obvious.'

Jason's own problems were pushed to the back of his mind for the time being. 'Where do you sleep?' he asked.

'Sleep? All over really. You know? Where we can. Not always on the trains, like. Sometimes we have to sleep rough in the stations. I hate that. It's freezing some nights. But I've slept hidden on the luggage racks above the seats, yeah? And in cupboards in the buffet. Anywhere. Just so long as you're not seen.' All the time the boy spoke he was constantly fidgeting, looking up and down the buffet car.

Jason felt as if that's exactly what he should have been doing too, but was more interested in the boy's story than anything else.

'What happens if you're caught?'

Jam shrugged. 'I've been caught twice so far. Was caught last month, yeah? No sweat though. Not really. They just send you back to the home, or to fosters again, yeah? Wherever. But it's easy to escape. Trouble is when the conductors get to know you, like. Some are OK. Some help you, don't grass you up. It's ones like Burkey you've got to watch out for.'

Jason was truly amazed. He'd never dreamed of people like Jam.

'It's good on trains,' the Runner

continued. 'Once you know how. Better than being on the streets. That's for mugs. At least trains are warm. And you can always get washed, yeah? Easy to steal food from the buffet, or those kiosks they've got at the stations. I've been all over the place you know? London and Wales. Edinburgh, too. Could go to France probably. Through the tunnel, if I

felt like it. No one to tie you down, tell you what to do. You're free like this, yeah?'

Jason nodded. 'Yeah.' He was about to say more, but didn't have a chance. Jam had suddenly grabbed him.

'Burkey!'

Jason looked over his shoulder, and sure enough there was Burkey the conductor walking along the corridor. He

was a tall man, walking with massive
strides towards them in his dark uniform,
there wasn't even the tiniest hint of a sway
from side to side. Jason's heart started to
thump quickly in his chest. Burkey's conductor cap was pushed down hard on his
head, and only grey, wirey sideburns
poked out from underneath. He had a
moustache the same colour, like a scouring

pad on his top lip. Jason felt his heart rise up into his throat as the man walked towards them. He definitely didn't want Jam to get caught now.

But Jam knew what to do. He pulled Jason over to the pay phone round the side of the buffet's counter and snatched up the receiver. He turned his back on Burkey and put one hand up over his ear

as if to block the noise of the Intercity, but really covering his face. He leaned right into the little plastic canopy above the phone. And he spoke as loudly as he could, almost shouting.

'Yeah, we should be on time, Mum. Don't worry. Tell Dad to pick us up, OK? Tell him we'll wait in the carpark at the usual place. Yeah, that's right. OK. See you later. Bye, Mum. Bye.'

And Burkey strode past them without a second glance.

Jam replaced the receiver and smiled full beam at Jason.

'Told you. No sweat. Easy when you know how.'

7 *The game*

THE TWO BOYS were sitting back down again. The Intercity dragged itself away from Manchester, although this time the houses never quite managed to fade away completely. The scenery was now mostly greys.

Jam had been telling stories from his days as a Runner. Like how he'd first met Burkey. He'd been the first conductor to catch him; caught him climbing into a luggage rack. And about how Jam had managed to stay one step ahead of him

ever since. Jason listened with an open mouth.

They were on the last leg of the journey. Not long before he could see Michael again. But he was beginning to wonder if going to see Michael was the right thing to do.

The Runner shrugged. 'Don't know who my mum and dad are. I was aban-

doned probably. Or given up when I was really young, yeah? Can't remember. Lived in homes all my life. Until I became a Runner, like.'

Jason was on the verge of telling Jam everything. He wanted to admit that he really was running away.

'I don't need a mum and dad anyway. No one does if you ask me. Not really.

I've had friends who've left homes, gone to live with families, yeah? And they've hated it. Can't stand all the rules and stuff. And one kid's new parents just argued all the time. All they did was shout at each other, he said. You know, swearing and stuff? So he left them. Walked right out. Came back to the home.' He looked at Jason and tapped his chest. 'That's why I've never gone with a new mum and dad, yeah? I've always put them off me. Made them not want to take me. Can't do with all the arguments, you know?'

Jason nodded. He knew.

'I think you only really need yourself,' Jam told him. 'That's what I think.

Everybody else just lets you down, yeah? Look at me. I've been doing fine for two years now. I haven't got flies on me, have I?' He shook his head to answer his own question. 'I'm a Runner, yeah? I don't need anybody. I bet Tommy Red doesn't neither. We can look after ourselves. It's what Runners do, yeah?'

Jason was quiet. Jam was staring out of the window, satisfied he'd made his point.

Maybe the Runner is right, Jason was thinking. Maybe watching out for yourself and not relying on others is the answer. He imagined what it would be like for him to live as Jam did, hopping from train to train. He imagined what it would be like not having anyone to

tie you down, not having anyone to *let* you down.

He thought about his parents. They'd betrayed him with all of their arguments and shouting, by not being happy. They'd hurt him, bad enough to make him cry at night. He didn't need them.

He thought about Ben, his supposed best friend. If he was as good a friend as

he always claimed to be then Jason would
have told him the truth about what he
was doing today, wouldn't he? But he'd
had to lie to Ben because he hadn't trust-
ed him not to grass him up. And the more
he thought about it, the more he began to
believe he really was alone. The more he
began to realise the only person he could
rely on was himself. Just like Jam said.

Maybe if Michael had truly loved him he wouldn't have gone to Liverpool and left him alone. He hadn't had to take a job so far away. So maybe it was time Jason learned to rely on himself. Maybe it was time he became a Runner too.

'At last. There you are.'

The voice made the two boys jump. Jam quite a bit higher than Jason.

'Your father and I have been looking for you *everywhere*.'

Jason looked round quickly to see a scary, moon-faced lady leaning over the two of them. He noticed she was frowning. She tutted. She had shiny, blonde hair piled high on top of her head, not one strand of it was out of place. Her make-up gave her face an odd orange tint, but her teeth were a purely natural yellow.

Jason turned to look at Jam, whose head was hung low.

'We weren't doing anything wrong,' the young boy said into his lap. 'Just playing. I wasn't being a nuisance. I'm not being any trouble. Honest I'm not.'

'Well you can come back straight away. You know what your father's like when he's in a mood, and I'm certain I don't want to suffer one of those today.' She fluttered her eyelashes with a sharp annoyance. 'Come along now, James. Quickly please, young man.' She beckoned him out of his seat with an impatient hand.

Jam squeezed his way past Jason, who didn't know what on earth to say. The young boy looked tiny by the side of the woman.

'Say good-bye to your little friend, James,' the lady ordered, even though she hadn't acknowledged Jason herself.

And Jam turned to Jason. He looked sad. He looked very young.

'Thank you for playing with me,' he said quietly, still looking at the floor. He offered his hand for Jason to shake it.

Jason shook hands. He'd never done it before and for some reason it made him feel older. The lady took hold of Jam's other hand and started to lead him away. But the small boy held on to Jason for that little while longer.

He brought his head up and met Jason's eyes. 'It was a good game, wasn't it?' he asked. 'Fun, yeah? You enjoyed it?'

Jason nodded slowly.

'Me too,' Jam told him. Then let his mother lead him away.

8 *End of the line*

JASON WAS WAITING by the door with his bag in his hand as the Intercity pulled into Liverpool. He was the first out on to the platform. He was looking for Jam but was soon caught up in the crowd of people as they flooded out after him. He tried to walk among them, pushing in between their legs and their

luggage. But he couldn't see Jam anywhere. People shook their heads and tutted at him when he got in their way. One
man purposely knocked him aside with
the heavy swing of a briefcase. Jam was
nowhere to be seen.

The crowd jostled him towards the exit.
And that was when he saw his brother,
waving, walking against the crowd on the

platform. He shouted Jason's name and hurried over.

Jason ran to meet him. He was so glad Michael still looked like he remembered. He'd been a bit worried that maybe –

'Mum and Dad thought you'd be coming here,' Michael said, interrupting his thoughts, and Jason knew that he didn't know whether to smile or scold

him. 'The school phoned Mum at work when you didn't appear after your *dentist appointment*. And Dad phoned me.'

'You're not angry are you?'

Michael still didn't look too sure. He shrugged. 'I don't know about Mum and Dad, but – well, I suppose you got me the day off work, so it can't be all bad, can it?' He took Jason's bag from him. He

looked serious now. 'You know you've given the two of them a bit of a shock, don't you? I reckon you've made them realise they're not the only ones with a couple of problems. They're coming up tomorrow so we can all sit down and have a long talk about things.'

Jason looked at his feet. He shivered a little in Liverpool's chill breeze.

'Dad been playing his awful music too loud again, has he?' Michael asked.

Jason nodded, and managed a smile even though he felt tears pricking at the backs of his eyes. 'I met a boy on the train,' he told his brother.

'He wasn't running away too, was he?'

Jason wasn't sure how to answer, because although Jam had been with his parents all along, he had still been doing his best to escape.

'Mum and Dad aren't all that bad,' Michael told him gently. 'Their arguments aren't the end of the world, really. You know that, don't you?'

Jason nodded. He was begining to figure that one out for himself.

His brother put his arm round his shoulders. 'Come on,' he said. 'Let's go to my flat and put some decent music on the stereo.'

But Jason didn't follow right away. He took one last look around the bustling train station. He wanted to find Jam. He wanted to tell him that it was OK to want to escape now and again. He wanted to tell him that he reckoned everyone did, sometimes.